#BeBrazen
BRAZEN FOLK HORROR

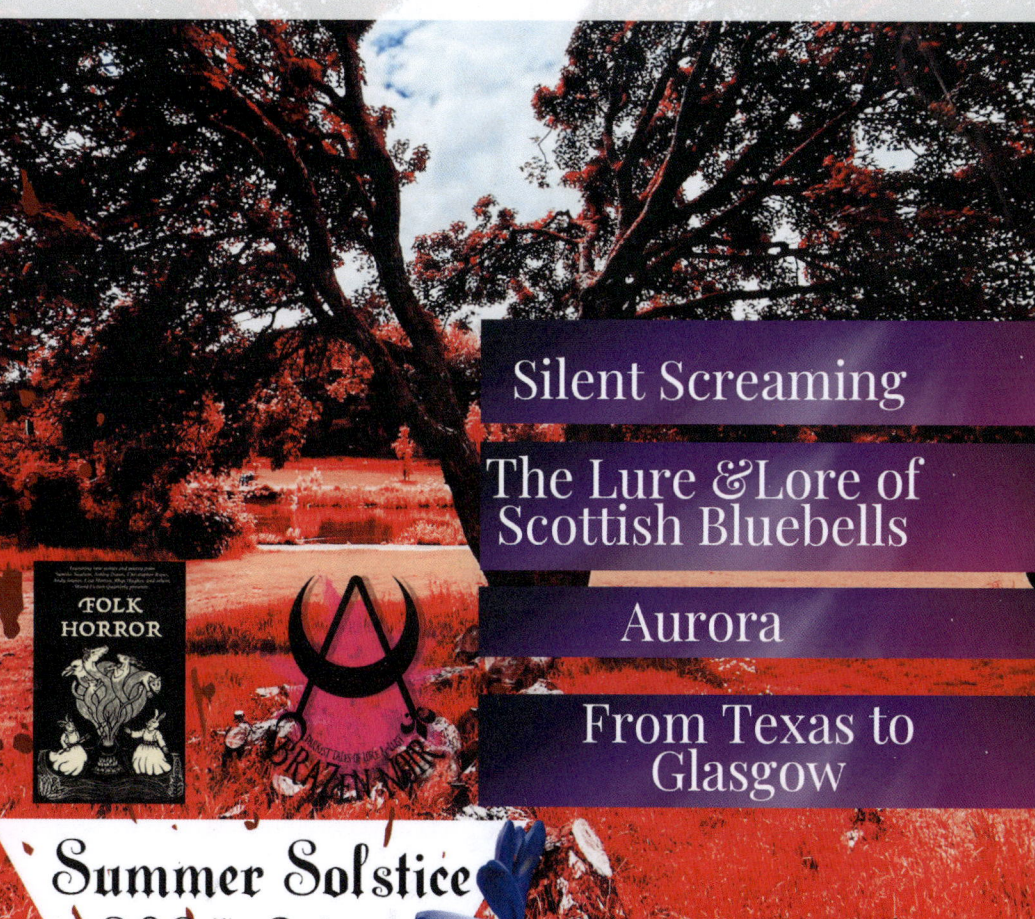

Silent Screaming

The Lure & Lore of Scottish Bluebells

Aurora

From Texas to Glasgow

Summer Solstice 2024 Edition

ISSUE 5

#BeBrazen

© 2024 Brazen folk Horror,
Ruthann Jagge & Natasha Sinclair

All rights reserved. This publication or any portion thereof including all images, may not be reproduced or used in any manner whatsoever without the express written permission of the author and publisher, except for the use of brief quotations in a book review. Any unauthorised use will constitute as an infringement of copyright.

ONLINE EDITION IS STICTLY SUBSCRIBER CONTENT ONLY. NOT FOR DISTRIBUTION WITHOUT EXPLICIT WRITTEN CONSENT FROM BRAZEN FOLK HORROR

Sign up: https://brazenfolkhorror.com
Contact: BrazenFolkHorror@Gmail.com

Graphic design, layout etc. by Natasha Sinclair
Cover Photography by Natasha Sinclair

All content, unless otherwise stated, are the work of Natasha Sinclair & Ruthann Jagge.

Original cover art for the Delevan trilogy was by Don Noble, Rooster Republic Press.

Published by Brazen Folk Horror. 2024
ISBN: 9798329034219

ISSUE 5   SUMMER SOLSTICE 2024

#BeBrazen

CONTENTS

WELCOME!

ABOUT BRAZEN FOLK HORROR

SUMMER SOLSTICE

THE LURE & LORE OF SCOTTISH BLUEBELLS

WE'RE OURSELVES

AURORA

WEE BITES OF FOLK

BRAZEN NOIR TEASE: SILENT SCREAMING

JUST A CAT

FROM TEXAS TO GLASGOW PART 2

BRAZEN READERS

ISSUE 5   SUMMER SOLSTICE 2024

#BeBrazen

WELCOME TO ISSUE 5!

Welcome, and thank you for joining us!

At Brazen Folk Horror neither Sinclair nor Jagge colour inside the lines. For our newsletter, it will only ever #BeBrazen.

Subscribers should expect #BeBrazen quarterly – on Solstice and Equinox. Packed with just enough fresh content to satisfy and be eager to feast on the next installment. Welcome to the Summer Solstice 2024 Edition!

With Magick and Mayhem,
Brazen Folk Horror

ISSUE 5   SUMMER SOLSTICE 2024

#BeBrazen

ABOUT BRAZEN FOLK HORROR

Brazen Folk Horror began as a friendship between two women over 6 thousand miles apart: Jagge on her ranch in Texas, USA and Sinclair in a wee village in the central belt of Scotland. Between the oceans blossomed camaraderie from a shared passion for crafting compelling, multidimensional characters and discovering the dark stories hiding in the shadows.

These two fearless women share a love of magical things and deep respect for history. The stories of Jagge and Sinclair have deep roots in folklore passed through the generations by great storytellers.

This pair enjoys sinking their claws deep into horror realism, eroticism, legends and mysticism without boundaries.

The brazen duo joined forces, each bringing their unique style to collaborate on the shamefully wicked tales readers crave under their brand, Brazen Folk Horror.

Ruthann Jagge

Natasha Sinclair

ISSUE 5   SUMMER SOLSTICE 2024

Scottish Proverb

A lie is half way roon Scotland afore the truth has its boots oan.

#BeBrazen

ISSUE 5   SUMMER SOLSTICE 2024

SUMMER SOLSTICE
JUNE 2024

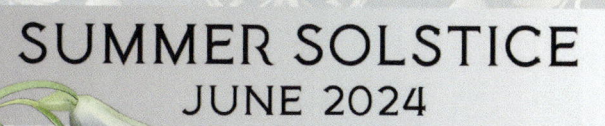

For thousands of years, humans around the Earth have celebrated the Solstices. The shifting elements and the rise and setting of the sun have long guided us. The longest day of the year has consistently been celebrated by the spiritually inclined and those who aren't in equal measure from the ancient world to the modern. We celebrate in rhythmic circles of song, chants, dance, ritual and connective touch. With many names, the Summer Solstice is also known as Midsummer and Litha (from the ancient Celts) among many pagans. This fire festival celebrates the fruitful and fertile Celtic Earth Goddess, Danu, who is also the mother of the fae — Túatha Dé Danaan. Litha also celebrates and mourns the death of the horned God of the hunt (born during Winter Solstice), Cernunnos. The Solstice celebrates in tandem the divine masculine and feminine energies— balance. We light bonfires to help the sun journey through the sky on the longest day, and those with

ISSUE 5   SUMMER SOLSTICE 2024

SUMMER SOLSTICE
JUNE 2024

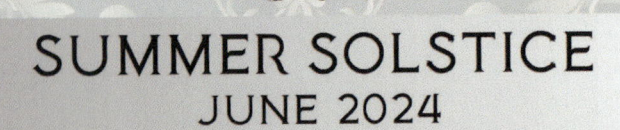

passion, courage and desire in their souls jump through the flames to claim blessings and luck. Hold your dreams to the light, or take a hand and share in the dreams of your circle and jump!

ISSUE 5   SUMMER SOLSTICE 2024

THE LURE & LORE OF SCOTTISH BLUEBELLS

"I lingered round them, under the benign sky; watched the moths fluttering among the heath and harebells; listened to the soft wind breathing through the grass; and wondered how anyone could ever imagine unquiet slumbers, for the sleepers in that quiet earth."

Emily Bronte
Wuthering Heights
published in 1847.

While cactus show off a bit — blooming with brilliant orange and yellow flowers against a mostly dry and brown background this time of the year in Texas, early spring into the month of June for the beautiful and fascinating bluebell in Scotland. A symbol of everlasting love for many.

The Scottish Bluebell is also known as harebell, bellflower, and fairy's thimble. The name, Harebell, has its roots in magick and folklore, subjects near to our hearts.

ISSUE 5   SUMMER SOLSTICE 2024

THE LURE & LORE OF SCOTTISH BLUEBELLS

Scottish Bluebells are frequently found growing in meadows frequented by rabbits and hare. Some would argue, the name Harebell was given this flower because certain types of witches were known to turn themselves into hares and hide among them. Both are interesting stories, one for the non-believer and believer. It's also suggested that fairies live among the flowers, and not always the charming sprites of Disney and light folklore. The more mischievous darker fae are whispered to dislike humans stomping on or picking the charming blooms, for fear they release a spell hidden inside. There are also those who refer to this sea of blue as the *Dead Man's Bells*. No doubt, rising from the belief that vindictive fairies cast spells on those who dare to trample on or pick the delicate blooms. It's frequently planted near precious cemetery markers and wild graves and the stunning Harebell is a favorite muse of poets over many years. Walter Gregory writes in *Notes on the Folklore of the North East of Scotland* (1881) that 'The bluebell (Campanula rotundifolia) is regarded with a sort of dread, and commonly left unpulled.' Likewise T F

ISSUE 5   SUMMER SOLSTICE 2024

THE LURE & LORE OF SCOTTISH BLUEBELLS

Thiselton-Dyer says in *The Folklore of Plants* (1889) 'Among further plants of ill omen may be mentioned the bluebell (Campanula rotundifolia), which in certain parts of Scotland was called *The aul' man's bell*, and was regarded with a sort of dread, and commonly left unpulled.' This may explain why the flowers were also called Dead Man's Bells. Interestingly the Scottish *aul' man* (old man) was another name given to the Devil. In traditional folktales fairies were often mischievous and dangerous creatures and therefore became linked with evil and the Devil.

If you're fortunate enough to find these flowers early in the morning, they may cast off an otherworldly violet glow, and are often found in circles. But take special care not to disturb or annoy any precious creature of folklore and myth and keep to the path to enjoy their sweet and seductive scent.

We at Brazen Folk horror believe, and tread lightly so as not to take away from the old ways.

ISSUE 5   SUMMER SOLSTICE 2024

WE'RE OURSELVES

Natasha and Ruthann were invited into Kandisha Press's Library to be interviewed as part of their Women In Horror series. Readers can find the interviews alongside other women working in the genre over on the blog: www.kandishapress.com/blog
Don't forget to support this excellent independent press when you visit by simply hitting subscribe!

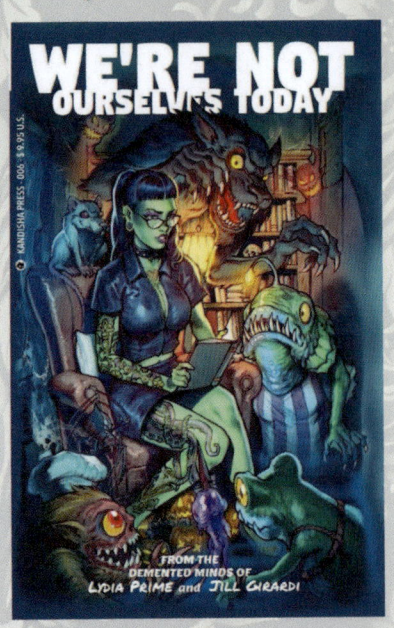

Also, check out their latest release, *We're Not Ourselves Today* - a pulp horror anthology of 13 original stories from Lydia Prime and Jill Girardi!

ISSUE 5   SUMMER SOLSTICE 2024

AURORA

The Aurora Borealis is a magical sight—one which fires imaginations and awe around the world. People chase the merry dancers, desperate for a glimpse of the geomagnetic storms and solar flares from charged solar partials hitting the gasses of the planet's atmosphere, which light up the skies with an otherworldly colourful luminescence that is, in fact, very much of the Earth. The Northern Lights, deeply woven into the fabric of various cultures' mythologies and folklore, hold a significant place. In Norse mythology, they were believed to be reflections of the Valkyrie's shields and armour. Some also saw them as the final breaths of fallen soldiers or the Bifrost Bridge to Valhalla. In Scottish Gaelic, they were known as Na Fil-Chlis — the Nimble Men in an eternal battle, with the aurora's crimson streaks representing the bloodshed. In many Northern American communities, the lights were seen as the souls of the departed - ancestors or hunted animals.

In Brazen Folk Horror's Delevan Trilogy, the mysticism of the Northern Lights acts as a doorway between the human world and Faerie. How could we not lean into this timeless Earth magick? This doorway is a natural catalyst that brings worlds together and divides them.

ISSUE 5   SUMMER SOLSTICE 2024

AURORA

It's not just us. Story tellers wielding a vast array of mediums continue to be inspired by the magick that pours from the great beyond, and this includes the more scientifically minded who understand the nuances of the solar winds colliding with Earth's magnetic field and the energy created within the ionosphere that create the 'magick' that inspires and captivates many of us veering out eyes upwards into the dancing night sky.

On May tenth, gazing from the wee pitched roof window of my bedroom, captivated by the gentle wisps of the sky. For the first time in my forty years, I witnessed the Aurora. I was spellbound by the Merry Dancers pouring the cloak of lights across the night sky. Poems and songs

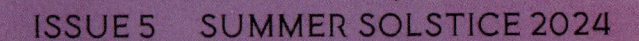

ISSUE 5   SUMMER SOLSTICE 2024

AURORA

swirled through my soul as I immersed myself in the wisps. Floating its soft tracks like hair in the breeze. I realised the cloud-like wisps were morphing in a way I had never witnessed before. I snatched my phone and swiped open the camera, and through the lens, the colours intensified. They spread like spilt watercolours, then deepened. I ran downstairs and barefoot out of my front door onto the empty village street and looked up, spinning in circles and laughing on the road. I snapped through the lens in one hand and let my eyes dive deep into the sky, mouth agape at the majesty and awe of witnessing this natural phenomenon over the head of my wee house for the first time.

When the world is dark, look up.
We never know what magick we may be blessed with in a few moments. Immerse in those beats. Dance in them, let them score soundtracks in your head and make you dizzy. And if another soul speaks to you, share the magick. These moments are agonisingly finite to the flesh in which we exist. Make them count.

AURORA

And with that here is a classic piece from Emily Dickinson — her 'Aurora'.

Aurora
Emily Elizabeth Dickinson

Of bronze and blaze
The north, to-night!
So adequate its forms,
So preconcerted with itself,
So distant to alarms, --
An unconcern so sovereign
To universe, or me,
It paints my simple spirit
With tints of majesty,
Till I take vaster attitudes,
And strut upon my stem,
Disdaining men and oxygen,
For arrogance of them.
My splendors are menagerie;
But their competeless show
Will entertain the centuries
When I am, long ago,
An island in dishonored grass,
Whom none but daisies know.

WEE BITES OF FOLK...
THEIR HORROR THAT IS

Weird Fiction Quarterly Presents Spring 2024:
Folk Horror Edition.

Featuring new stories and poetry from Sumiko Saulson, Ashley Dioses, Christopher Ropes, Andy Joynes, Lisa Morton, Rhys Hughes, and others, Weird Fiction Quarterly presents...

FOLK HORROR

From the Foreward by Shayne K. Keene, Editor:
"So, this is not a folk horror anthology for the purist but for those who would like to include all sorts of things that people have to deal with, most involving the supernatural. It was not our aim to challenge or change what folk horror is, but our writers, it seems, wouldn't have it any other way."

ISSUE 5   SUMMER SOLSTICE 2024

WEE BITES OF FOLK...
THEIR HORROR THAT IS

Natasha and I are devotees of this sub-genre in all forms, so when I had the opportunity to read the latest edition of Weird Fiction Quarterly dedicated to our favorite forms of literature rooted in lore, superstition, hearsay, or imagination, I was delighted. Primarily because this edition features the work of over sixty authors presented in tasty bites of flash fiction, which are insidiously challenging to write as they allow the use of only five hundred words to tell a complete story or craft a memorable poem — it is no small feat for the most seasoned of writers.

This collection is worthy of adding to the most diverse library shelves for the array of entertaining, sometimes perplexing, and vivid tales from authors of various backgrounds who design their versions of folk and horror in both the uniquely traditional and some impressively fresh styles. The history of what makes horror "of a

people" or "folk" is relevant and essential, as it is part of life's legacy. Still, it's fantastic to read stories from those who are writing from contemporary perspectives, thereby setting the pace for what may become "tradition" in the

WEE BITES OF FOLK... THEIR HORROR THAT IS

years ahead. I found the entire collection easy and fast to read but no less complex in the emotions these stories manage to tickle and poke at.

Some stories were simple in intention, while others were more indefinite in their intention and effect. It's a mixed bag of the familiar combined with stories that deserve to be read twice to understand the author's more singular inspirations. I can honestly say that I enjoyed and read every one included, but a few stood out to me as genuinely
representing the folk horror title in a remarkable way:

Four Stars Would Book Again by Kurt Fawver
We Give You Our Best, Our Most Cherished by Jill Hand
The Woodwose by Phil Breach
When They Came by Lisa Morton
The Well by Frances Lu-Pai Ippolito

It's impossible to choose a favorite, as I loved so many, but these resonated with me as exceptions in a collection where there are none to be ignored. It's an expertly curated and presented edition in paperback, punctuated

ISSUE 5   SUMMER SOLSTICE 2024

WEE BITES OF FOLK...
THEIR HORROR THAT IS

by moody interior illustrations by Sarah Walker. The entire tone and feel of the collection left me hungry for a walk in the woods beyond the pasture, yet with a wholly satisfying and nudging feeling that I probably should do so only during daylight hours.

This is an edition for every reader, from those who enjoy quick bites of horror that leave a mark to those more cerebral who wait until one leg falls out from the covers on a rainy night to remember why it's a bad idea to doubt what your grandmother may have whispered regarding the heavy wooden family heirloom of an armoire you inherited at the foot of your bed.

Grab this from wherever you prefer, but don't let it get away! I predict nominations for this collection once award season rolls around again.

This edition offers a lot of reading enjoyment, some solid scares, and even more talent in the pages between the stunning and evocative cover art by Liv Rainey-Smith.

Ruthann Jagge
For Brazen Folk Horror

WEE BITES OF FOLK...
THEIR HORROR THAT IS

Weird Fiction Quarterly is available at a wide variety of international sellers:

https://weirdfictionquarterly.com/weird-fiction-quarterly-folk-horror-2024-is-available

Featuring new stories and poetry from
Sumiko Saulson, Ashley Dioses, Christopher Ropes,
Andy Joynes, Lisa Morton, Rhys Hughes, and others,
Weird Fiction Quarterly presents...

FOLK HORROR

ISSUE 5   SUMMER SOLSTICE 2024

Silent Screaming

I told him where it hurt, he threw his mouth upon me, sucked hard and sunk in his teeth. My eyes filled, and I could have screamed. Blinded by tears and need. If I screamed, would he stop *Don't stop. Don't stop silence. It hurts, and I need the hurt.* I told him how another suffocated me, so he threw his hands around my throat and squeezed, never leaving my eyes. I watched his dead eyes fill with rage and hate for himself. I'm just an empty mirror—nothing to take personally at the hand of this lonely killer. Quietly, I choked and wondered how much harder he'd squeeze. I could take more. *Squeeze harder. Fuck me harder.*

When I said no, his demons had already blinded and taken his hearing. It's okay. I only say no to feed them. They're always starving and never sated. *Feed them. They need it. I am nothing. My need is needless to these dead men.* He forgot my name—it's okay 'good girl' can be anyone whose mouth envelops his cock. Lost boys are all the same.

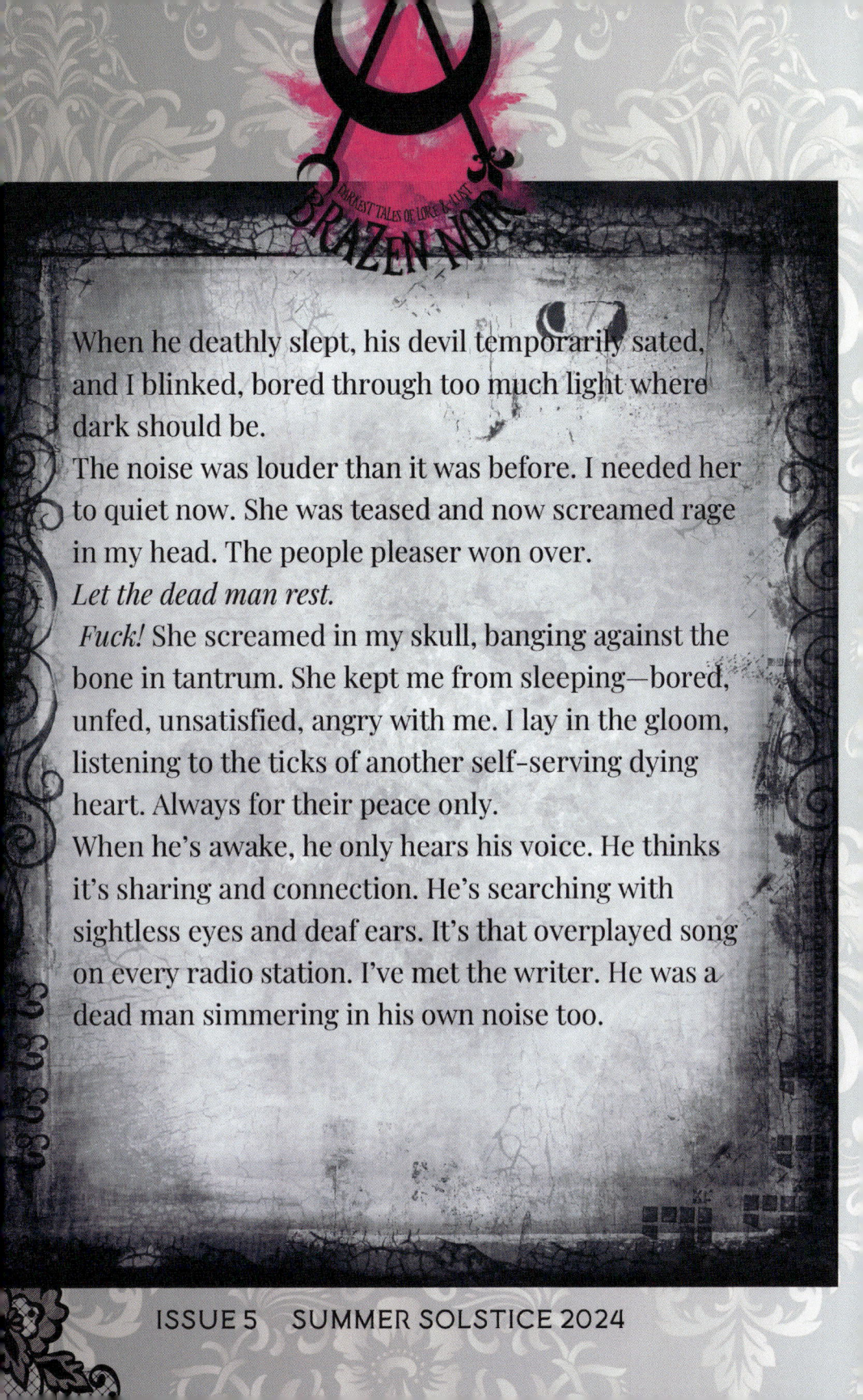

When he deathly slept, his devil temporarily sated, and I blinked, bored through too much light where dark should be.

The noise was louder than it was before. I needed her to quiet now. She was teased and now screamed rage in my head. The people pleaser won over.

Let the dead man rest.

Fuck! She screamed in my skull, banging against the bone in tantrum. She kept me from sleeping—bored, unfed, unsatisfied, angry with me. I lay in the gloom, listening to the ticks of another self-serving dying heart. Always for their peace only.

When he's awake, he only hears his voice. He thinks it's sharing and connection. He's searching with sightless eyes and deaf ears. It's that overplayed song on every radio station. I've met the writer. He was a dead man simmering in his own noise too.

If you mix the creeping dread of "The Wicker Man" with the mysterious elements of "Practical Magic", you have Delevan House. A curious and bewitching place rooted in dreadful history, superstition and sorcery with a legacy of dark secrets.

Delevan House is a brazenly executed contemporary story that brings fresh blood to the genres and timelines it crosses; breathing life into folklore and horror fantasy.

Set in the village of Badb, the hulking majesty of Delevan House has eyes everywhere, reflecting secrets of the old ways that are a necessary evil for survival.

This seductive and sophisticated gothic tale is rooted in Scottish folklore, dark history, and what we all desire – freedom.

Delevan House is where literal worlds collide. Lady Lenore Delevan is waiting.

Do you dare enter under the eyes of her menacing stone beast and obsidian flock?

ISSUE 5   SUMMER SOLSTICE 2024

Coming 2024

THE DELEVAN DIARIES

Trapped in Delevan House for centuries, Lady Lenore Delevan is now free.

The cost to Badb's villagers is grave. Their binding ritual spilled outsiders' blood. Many will suffer the consequences.

In The Delevan Diaries, ancient superstitions and insidious obligations unravel. Tensions rise between the villagers and the Travelling community who have come to collect.

In Elphame, the betrayed Dark Queen of the Unseelie, Nicnevin, with her terrible Sluagh na marbh, is also plotting retribution.

Book II of The Delevan trilogy continues to weave history, unforgettable characters, and Scottish mythology together in a contemporary gothic folk horror like no other.

Whose magicks and beliefs will survive?

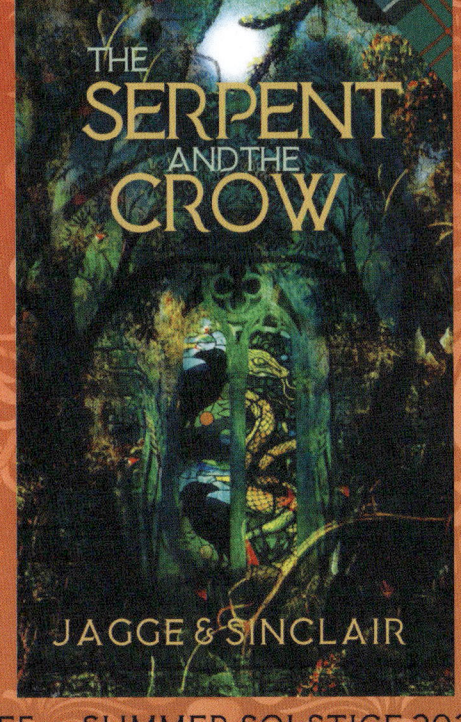

JAGGE & SINCLAIR

THE SERPENT AND THE CROW

JAGGE & SINCLAIR

ISSUE 5   SUMMER SOLSTICE 2024

JUST A CAT

What If?

I keep thinking, what if I've done wrong by him? What if he wasn't ready? What if his pain wasn't as bad as the noise he made when he cried out in his sleep? What if his body was changing, and it wasn't agony I saw on his face when he moved, and his back slumped? What if I left him continue to whither? What if he had lingered less than a half-life for a while longer? Would that have been kinder? More loving?

I saw my dear little love dwindle every day, spiralling to the bottom of the funnel. His confusion was greater than in lucid times. States were a series of blurred lines. He'd stumble and fall from a slight movement of his delicate paw. My little love cat would cry in his sleep and violently twitch in fright. (I remember an old friend of his who did that. Though, Gabriel's was far more violent —full-blown seizures that always left him soaking and often injured from the events. The terror that caused my little sensitive foundling to witness was heart-wrenching. I'd never let love suffer so.) Then there were moments when he'd be on me, my Loki and I, chest to chest, and he'd purr as he had for 18 years. There'd be light in place of pain.

JUST A CAT

What if I pulled the trigger too soon? What if I was wrong? And he trusted me....

What if I hadn't — and one of those convulsions turned into a fit that prolonged pain, and I couldn't get the help to end that suffering?

I never had it in me to use my own hands to end a life. I felt that coming...a painful end. I was certain it would be horrific. I could see it.

And yet, I'm riddled with grief and loss. I can't help but wonder...what if I was wrong? What if I didn't kill him? What if we held each other a little longer, my love cat and I?

Loki Sinclair 2006 - 2024

ISSUE 5   SUMMER SOLSTICE 2024

THE ROAD FROM TEXAS TO GLASGOW

And here we are, a mere two months from the epitome of squealing and mayhem. AKA…Ruthann goes to Scotland.

Am I even remotely close to being ready to travel six thousand miles ensconced in a tiny pod under Delta Airline's "trusted" wings?

Nope. But it isn't stopping me from trying to plot and plan almost non-stop.

I've secured the host hotel for the WorldCon convention, and a few other lovely places to eat and sleep as well. We've been awarded a coveted table in the Vendor's room and will have some of our work on display. We'll be the tall redhead and petite brunette over in the corner giggling non-stop, kind of like the Owens sisters in Practical Magic. I did not say we'd be casting spells, get your mind out of the, but hey…you never know?

www.glasgow2024.org

www.sec.co.uk

ISSUE 5   SUMMER SOLSTICE 2024

THE ROAD FROM TEXAS TO GLASGOW

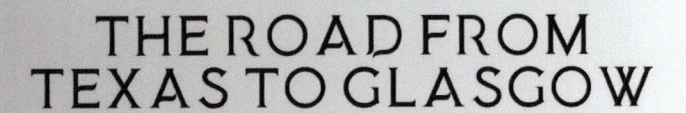

The event promises to be extraordinary, and the vast array of offerings over the five days the convention runs is truly mind-boggling. I've attended several major literary conventions, but this one is a doozy, and my first international one.

I want to experience Natasha's exciting hometown of Glasgow, and the visually stunning Edinburgh. Did I mention there's also a little party going on there during the month of August called The Fringe Festival? It attracts thousands, on top of the thousands expected for Worldcon so it must be said, that I've chosen a hell of a month to be in central Scotland. My naturally reclusive tendencies will need to be shrugged off beforehand, as there will be a lot of people to meet and enjoy.

If I'm going the distance, I'm going all out! I'll need to make a return-trip to extend my steps to the farther reaches of this beautiful country, but I intend to take as many of the sights, sounds, food, music, and even indulge a bit in the local libations as well.

ISSUE 5   SUMMER SOLSTICE 2024

THE ROAD FROM TEXAS TO GLASGOW

I'm counting down the days to be able to spend time with one of my favorite people, and possibly a few other U.K. friends too. I keep changing up my packing list as I'm used to the hot and hotter climate of south Texas in the summer and have been advised to be prepared for anything!

I think folks are referring to the weather, but it's going to be the ultimate opportunity for us to #bebrazen in all our glory, jetlag and crowds be dammed.

I fully intend to chronicle, take photos, and despite our general disdain of social media, we'll be updating and sharing probably more than we need to be.

After all, when you're in the land of so many mythical creatures, and ripe history, who knows what might happen?

Hey...it worked for Claire in Outlander and although I have a loving partner, one shouldn't ever turn up her nose at an eighteenth century kilted Scottish Highlander?

Stay tuned for much more to come, I'm literally giddy and terrified at the same time over what's ahead!

Look for the hashtag #redheadritesinscotland because it's going to be entertaining at the very least.

ISSUE 5   SUMMER SOLSTICE 2024

BRAZEN READERS

Without you, we are just screaming into an empty void. We appreciate every single one of you. Whether you've read a little or consumed it all, thank you for joining our brazen flock. To name a few...

Dawn Keate, Rachel Schommer, RJ Roles, Dave Simms, Jason Myers, Jill Girardi, Paul Fegan, Mike Jagge, Fiona Angus (RIP, you immensley beautiful soul), Nat Whiston, Ben Eades, Mark Young, Kevin J. Kennedy, Stacy Layne Wilson, Erica Fields, Heidi Hess, Sally Feliz, Colton Skinner, Tiffany Koplin, Rocky Colavito, Lauren Kelson, Rachel Coffman, Milt Theo, John Palisano, Gwen Sergent, Sam, Vincent, Heath, Kim Hamilton, Chris Bonner, Derek Thomas, Angel Harrison, Brandy Carroll, The Demigod, Fiona, Mikki, Chris McAuley, Jossi Stevens, Mhairi Jane, Rebecca, Mary, Grant Flavell, Emma McKay, Joanne, Patrick, Luna, Andrew, Hilary, Scott, and you!

ISSUE 5   SUMMER SOLSTICE 2024

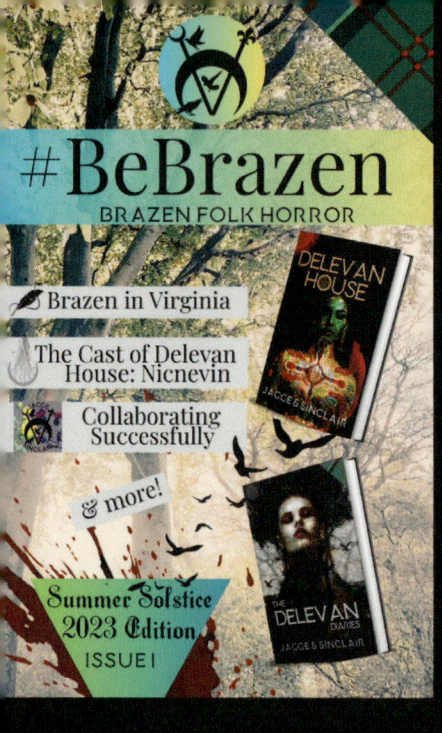

#BeBrazen
BRAZEN FOLK HORROR

- Brazen in Virginia
- The Cast of Delevan House: Nicnevin
- Collaborating Successfully
- & more!

Summer Solstice 2023 Edition
ISSUE 1

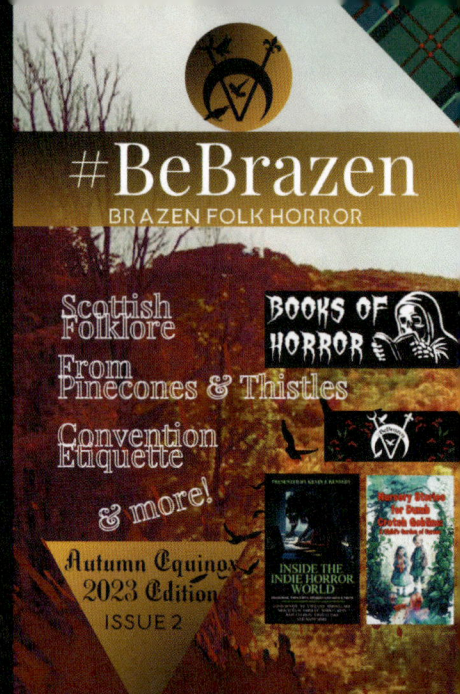

#BeBrazen
BRAZEN FOLK HORROR

- Scottish Folklore
- From Pinecones & Thistles
- Convention Etiquette
- & more!

BOOKS OF HORROR

Autumn Equinox 2023 Edition
ISSUE 2

#BeBrazen
BRAZEN FOLK HORROR

- The Art and Honour of Foreword Writing
- Stories in the Walls
- Six Thousand Miles
- The Delevan Diaries: First Look
- & More!

Winter Solstice 2023 Edition
ISSUE 3

#BeBrazen
BRAZEN FOLK HORROR

- Metamorphosis
- March of Women: History and Horror
- Brazen Noir Teaser

Spring Equinox 2024 Edition
ISSUE 4

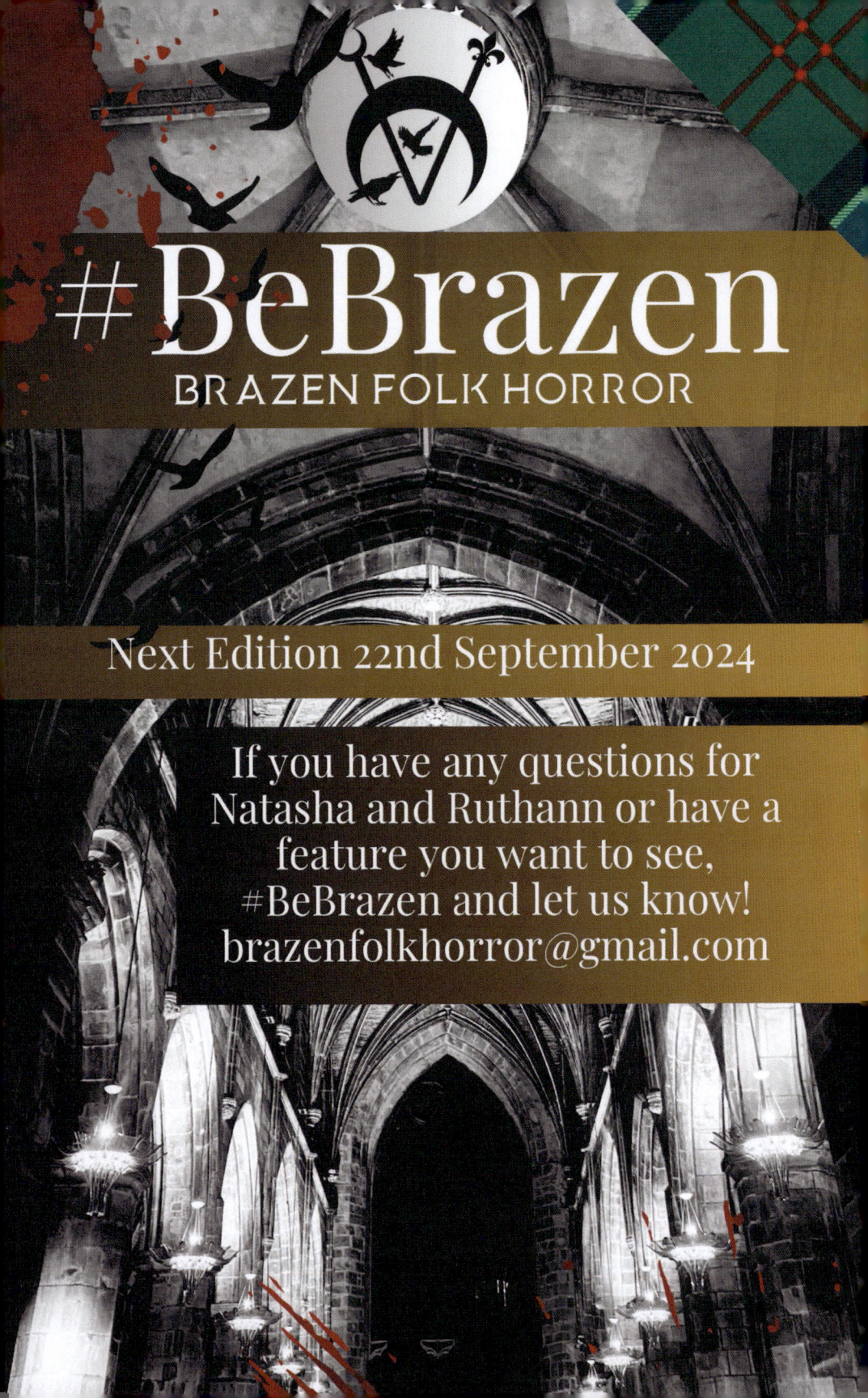

#BeBrazen
BRAZEN FOLK HORROR

Next Edition 22nd September 2024

If you have any questions for Natasha and Ruthann or have a feature you want to see, #BeBrazen and let us know!
brazenfolkhorror@gmail.com

#BeBrazen
BRAZEN FOLK HORROR

BrazenFolkHorror.com

Printed in Great Britain
by Amazon